Hans Brinker

inspired by the novel by

MARY MAPES DODGE

retold by BRUCE COVILLE

illustrated by LAUREL LONG

Dial Books for Young Readers

For Lauri Hornik —B.C.
For my sister Denise —L.L.

"Hans! Have you heard? There's to be a great race!" Gretel Brinker's eyes flashed as she skated up to her brother. "And the prize is a pair of silver skates, one for the boys, one for the girls! Hans, do you think we could win?"

"Not on these skates," he replied.

Hans and Gretel loved to skate. But their father had been badly hurt in an accident ten years earlier. Now the family was so poor that the children's skates were made of wood—not at all fit for racing.

"Such ragbags shouldn't be allowed to race at all," sneered Carl Schummel, who was listening nearby.

"Oh, Carl," sighed Annie Baumann. Then, knowing that Hans would never accept charity, she skated to him and said, "Hans, would you make me a wooden chain like the beautiful one you carved for Gretel?" Cleverly, the price Annie offered was just that of a pair of good skates.

$\mathcal{H}$ans and Gretel almost had a fight over who should have the new skates. But since the money had been earned by Hans, he got to choose—which meant the skates went to Gretel! Soon she was skimming across the ice like a merry sunbeam.

Even so, Hans did not have to wait long for skates of his own, since Annie's friend Peter decided *his* sister must also have a wooden chain, and paid Hans to make one.

As Hans prepared to set out for Amsterdam to buy his new skates, he noticed a sad look on Dame Brinker's face. Taking her hands, he said, "What troubles you, Mother?"

She glanced toward her husband's sleeping form. "I miss your father's laugh more than usual at holiday time. And . . . well, it is hard to be poor. Especially when . . ."

"When what?"

Dame Brinker sighed. "It is time you knew, Hans. Before your father was injured we had saved a thousand guilders. Then one day Raff came to me with a silver watch. 'Wife,' he said, 'I need you to guard this.' I agreed, of course, though I was curious about where it came from.

"That night a great storm arose and your father was called to work on the dikes." Dame Brinker looked away. "That was when he was injured, Hans. In my sorrow, I comforted myself by thinking, At least the children and I will have the thousand guilders to live on until Raff heals. But the money had vanished!" Her lip trembled. "All our work, gone! Did your father spend the money on that watch? I cannot imagine him being so foolish! But where did it go? And where did the watch come from?" She shook her head. "Tonight is St. Nicholas Eve. Go buy your skates, my son. I will put on my holiday clothes, and we will make a merry time of it yet!"

Hans headed for Amsterdam, his heart heavy with his mother's story.

"Hey, Ragbag!" shouted Carl Schummel, when he saw Hans walk by. "Keep those skates over your shoulder. They're not fit to be on the ice."

Hans flushed and sped away toward Amsterdam. Shortly after he reached the city he spied a doctor famous for both his brilliance and his bad temper. Suddenly Hans knew what he had to do with his money. Gathering his courage, he approached the great doctor.

"Mynheer Boekman, I must ask a favor."

"Out of the way, boy. I never give to beggars!"

"I'm no beggar!" declared Hans. He pulled out his money. "See? I can pay. I wish to consult you about my father."

The doctor was struck by something in Hans's eyes. His voice softer now, he said, "Put away your money, boy. I will see your father when I am able."

Hans told the doctor where they lived. Then, filled with new hope, he went to buy his skates.

*T*hat night, as children all over Holland prepared for the visit of St. Nicholas, Hans and Gretel frolicked on the moonlit ice. Though they skated past houses that held great feasts, they were happy in their small treasures—until they heard a cry of fear from their own cottage.

Rushing home, they found their father caught in a strange fit. He was gripping his wife with the strength of a dying man and they had fallen near the fire. Frantically, Hans and Gretel pulled Raff away from their mother. He collapsed into a restless sleep from which they could not wake him.

To the family's great relief, Dr. Boekman arrived the next morning. But soon the doctor presented them with a painful choice: "I know an operation that may help this man, but it is risky and I cannot promise he will live through it."

Dame Brinker murmured a prayer, then gave her consent.

The doctor turned to Hans. "I will need your help, lad. Can I depend on you?"

Despite his terror, Hans nodded solemnly.

As Dr. Boekman took his glittering instruments from their case, Gretel fled the cottage. Hans longed to join her but could not; he knew his place was at the doctor's side.

It took hours to finish the delicate task. A hush hung over the cottage as Hans and his mother waited in an agony of hope and fear to learn if the operation was a success. But at last Raff began to whisper, "Steady, boys! The water's rising . . ."

Dame Brinker sprang forward. "Raff!"

His eyes fluttered open. "Is that you, wife? Where are Hans and Gretel?"

"Here I am, Father!" said Hans.

"And I," cried Gretel, running into the cottage.

Raff stared at his children in astonishment, and Hans could sense how sad and strange it was for his father to wake and find his little boy a sturdy lad of fifteen, his baby daughter a beautiful girl of twelve, his young wife a woman of middle age. "So many years," Raff moaned.

"The danger is not over," Dr. Boekman warned them. "Dame Brinker, your husband must rest. And he must not become agitated!"

The doctor prescribed white bread, fresh meat, and wine for Raff's health. But such things had not been seen by the Brinkers since they'd fallen into poverty. Dame Brinker was tempted to sell the mysterious watch, yet she could not bring herself to defy the last wish her husband had uttered before his injury. And she dared not mention the watch for fear of upsetting Raff and driving him back into illness.

Hans was bolder. Sitting by his father's side, he cleverly led Raff to speak of the money.

"I buried it because our neighbor said something that made me mistrust him." Suddenly Raff's face grew troubled. "Did I tell your mother where I hid the money, Hans? Oh, I must have! How else could you have survived all these years?"

Rather than tell Raff that the money had never been found, Hans asked gently, "What clever place did you bury it, Father? I was too little to help mother dig it up."

"Just south of that willow behind the cottage," murmured Raff as he drifted back into sleep.

That night Hans and his mother dug for hours around the willow. But there was no money to be found.

The next day, Hans heard his mother say, "Raff, tell me about this." The boy went to stand nearby as his father studied the mysterious watch.

Finally Raff nodded as if remembering.

"I was working on the canal when a young man rushed up to me, desperate to go down the line. I agreed to take him. As I rowed, he began to sob. 'A man is dead,' he wept, 'and I must flee. But I am innocent!' Just before he left the boat he said, 'Take this watch to my father! Tell him if he wants me back, I'll brave prison to come. Tell him write to . . . to . . .'"

Raff's voice faltered. "I cannot remember!" He groaned. "I cannot even remember the name of his father! Oh, the poor lad!"

When Hans went outside to tell Gretel what he had heard, he found her talking to Annie Baumann. The two were so lovely in the December twilight that Hans said, "You look like a pair of winter fairies!"

Springing from the willow stump where she had been sitting, Annie declared, "Then I shall grant you a wish!"

"I wish I could find what I sought last night," said Hans boldly.

Annie stamped her foot three times. Slipping her hand into her pocket, she found a glass bead. Passing it to Hans, she said, "Bury this where I have stamped, and your wish will be granted."

Though Annie spoke in play, it was as if a magic had come over her. She had given Hans the answer to the mystery.

"Don't you see, Mother?" he asked that night, as he dug where Annie had stood. "This stump was the tree father spoke of. The tree where we dug last night was but a sapling when he was injured." He stopped, then gasped, "Look!"

There they were—the lost thousand guilders!

Dr. Boekman's next visit was the day before the big race. When he arrived at the cottage, Raff eagerly offered to pay him.

"Tut tut," replied the doctor kindly. "Hans's thanks was reward enough for me."

Dame Brinker smiled. "I suspect you have a son too!"

Alarmed by the doctor's sudden scowl, Raff moved to change the subject. "Forgive my wife. It's just that she has been worried about another lad of late, a lad we wish to help." With this, out came the mysterious watch—and with it, another surprise: The young man Raff had helped was Dr. Boekman's son!

"Poor Laurens!" said the doctor. "He was my helper, and one day he prepared the wrong medicine for a patient. I spotted the error, so the medicine was never given, but the man died anyway. Before I could tell Laurens it wasn't his fault, he had fled. Think, Raff! Where did Laurens say I should send for him?"

Raff rubbed his brow. "Figgs. Wiggs. I don't know. The name is gone!"

"I will find your son, mynheer!" said Hans. "I will devote every day of my life to the search."

Dr. Boekman patted his arm. "No, stay close to your father, Hans. At any moment, he may remember more. And when you race tomorrow— race for me!"

The next day it seemed as if all Holland had gathered on the ice! Rich and poor, old and young, city folk and country dwellers, all came together in a mad array of styles and costumes.

Twenty boys and twenty girls were to race. The course was a half mile down the ice, then straight back. The first skater in each group to win twice would receive the silver skates.

The girls went first. Blades sparkling, they seemed to fly down the ice. As they started back, one came on like an arrow, whizzing past the others.

Gretel Brinker had won the first heat!

Now it was the boys' turn. Hans and Peter raced well, but scornful Carl Schummel came in first.

Again the girls lined up. Again they flashed down the ice, but this time Annie Baumann won.

The boys again. Hans raced well, but it was Peter who first crossed the line.

Once more the girls set out, skimming over the ice like a flock of colorful birds. And ahead of them all came Gretel, winning the race, and with it the silver skates!

Hans turned to see if Peter had witnessed this victory. But his friend was trying to fix a broken skate strap.

Hans hurried to Peter's side. "Here! Take mine!" Peter tried to push him off, but Hans insisted. "I could not win, Peter. The race is between you and Carl. Take the strap!"

And so it was that Peter, not Hans, won the race.

That night Hans and Gretel were admiring Gretel's skates, and the fine leather case that held them. On the case, in sparkling letters, was written, "For the Fleetest."

Below those words were smaller letters.

Hans strained to read them. "Ah!" he said at last. "It is the maker of the case: Thomas Higgs, of Birmingham."

Raff sat up, his eyes wide. "Higgs!" he cried. "Higgs! That is the name the doctor's son gave me!"

The next moment Hans was racing to Dr. Boekman with the wonderful news that his son had been found.

In but a few days, Laurens was back at his father's side.

As the years went by, the two families remained close. And when the day came that Hans was old enough, Dr. Boekman invited him to come and work as his new assistant.

In good time, Hans Brinker became one of Holland's finest doctors—and also one of the kindest. For even as a great man, he never forgot what it was to be poor, and in need.

A Note from the Adaptor

Though *Hans Brinker, or The Silver Skates* is a much beloved book, it is perhaps more loved than actually read these days.

In a way, the novel is a victim of technology. When Mary Mapes Dodge (1831–1905) first published the story in 1865, it offered a marvelous way to present children with information about another country. In her preface Dodge admitted her didactic intent, saying, "This little work aims to combine the instructive features of a book of travels with the interest of a domestic tale." But the Internet now offers so many ways to learn about a place like Holland that those "instructive features," which once might have been so interesting, now stand in the way of the story. (Indeed, at one point the novelist abandons Hans for the better part of a hundred pages to detail a trip to Amsterdam made by some of his friends!)

The thing is, underneath the book's wealth of social, geographical, and historical data pulses a charming and quite moving story about a family struggling to thrive against great odds. It is this story that Laurel Long and I have tried to bring to the forefront in our adaptation.

There is another important aspect of *Hans Brinker* that I would like to mention, an aspect that may appear as dated as the information overload to some adults, but that I believe is vital for young readers, and that is the character of Hans himself. In our cynical age the boy seems almost too good to be true. But the fact is that the hearts of children yearn for such goodness, yearn for role models. In this regard Hans Brinker—both story and character—fills a deep emotional need. As Bruno Bettelheim says in *The Uses of Enchantment:* "The question for the child is not, 'Do I want to be good?' but 'Who do I want to be like?'"

It is here, most of all, that the story created by Mary Mapes Dodge has so much to offer. For I cannot help but believe that our world would be a better place indeed were it populated by more people as strong of heart and true of purpose as sturdy Hans Brinker.

—*Bruce Coville*

DIAL BOOKS FOR YOUNG READERS
A division of Penguin Young Readers Group • Published by The Penguin Group
Penguin Group (USA) Inc., 375 Hudson Street, New York, NY 10014, U.S.A.

Penguin Group (Canada), 90 Eglinton Avenue East, Suite 700, Toronto, Ontario, Canada • M4P 2Y3 (a division of
Pearson Penguin Canada Inc.) • Penguin Books Ltd, 80 Strand, London WC2R 0RL, England • Penguin Ireland, 25
St. Stephen's Green, Dublin 2, Ireland (a division of Penguin Books Ltd) Penguin Group (Australia), 250 Camber-
well Road, Camberwell, Victoria 3124, Australia (a division of Pearson Australia Group Pty Ltd) • Penguin Books
India Pvt Ltd, 11 Community Centre, Panchsheel Park, New Delhi - 110 017, India • Penguin Group (NZ), Cnr
Airborne and Rosedale Roads, Albany, Auckland 1310, New Zealand (a division of Pearson New Zealand Ltd) •
Penguin Books (South Africa) (Pty) Ltd, 24 Sturdee Avenue, Rosebank, Johannesburg 2196, South Africa • Penguin
Books Ltd, Registered Offices: 80 Strand, London WC2R 0RL, England

Designed by Nancy R. Leo-Kelly
Text set in Hoeffler Text
Manufactured in China on acid-free paper
3 5 7 9 10 8 6 4 2

Library of Congress Cataloging-in-Publication Dataw

Coville, Bruce.
Hans Brinker / inspired by the novel by Mary Mapes Dodge ; retold by Bruce Coville ; illustrated by Laurel Long.
p. cm.
Summary: A Dutch brother and sister work toward two goals, finding the doctor who can restore
their father's memory and winning the competition for the silver skates.
ISBN-13: 978-0-8037-2868-4
[1. Brothers and sisters—Fiction. 2. Ice skating—Fiction. 3. Netherlands—Fiction. 4. Long, Laurel, ill.]
I. Dodge, Mary Mapes, 1831–1905. Hans Brinker. II. Title.
PZ7.C8344Han 2007 [E]Z—dc22 2006027109

The art for this book was created using oil paints on watercolor paper primed with gesso.